MONSTER
and Boy

MONSTER and *Boy*

THE SISTER SURPRISE

Hannah Barnaby

Illustrated by Anoosha Syed

GODWINBOOKS

Henry Holt and Company
New York

Henry Holt and Company, *Publishers since 1866*
Henry Holt® is a registered trademark of Macmillan Publishing Group, LLC
120 Broadway, New York, NY 10271 · mackids.com

Library of Congress Control Number: 2021906626

ISBN 978-1-250-21787-5

Our books may be purchased in bulk for promotional, educational, or
business use. Please contact your local bookseller or the Macmillan
Corporate and Premium Sales Department at (800) 221-7945 ext. 5442 or
by e-mail at MacmillanSpecialMarkets@macmillan.com.

First edition, 2021 / Designed by Mallory Grigg
Printed in the United States of America by LSC Communications,
Crawfordsville, Indiana

10 9 8 7 6 5 4 3 2 1

For my brother, Andrew.
(Even though I asked for a sister.)
—H. B.

For my little monsters,
Zakaria and Mikael.
—A. S.

Hello again!

It is I, your friendly narrator. You probably remember me from the first Monster and Boy book and also from the second Monster and Boy book, which were stories that started a bit like this:

Once there was a monster who loved a boy. And a boy who loved a monster.

They hadn't always known each other. The monster lived under the boy's bed for a long time before they met, and the boy didn't know the

monster was there until one night
when the monster decided to introduce
himself. And now they were friends.

So far, the monster had swallowed
the boy and made him tiny and then
made him big again, and the boy
had taken the monster to school and
they had solved a mystery together
about roller skates and a
hedgehog. You know.
Typical friend stuff.

After their
day at school,
the monster
had learned
quite a lot, but he
still had questions
about many things.
One of those things
was names. That was
when he learned that the boy had a
name, and the boy's sister had a name.
She even had a *middle* name.

Does your middle have a name, too?

The monster did not have a name—
at least, not that he knew of—and he
had decided something.

He wanted a name of his own.

1.

One night, not long after their adventure at school, the monster and the boy were sitting in the boy's room. The monster, who was nocturnal (mostly), was very wide awake. The boy—who was not nocturnal (mostly)—was rather sleepy. But he was something else, too.

"You look grumpy," the monster told the boy.

"I *am* grumpy," the boy said.

"Is it because you don't have fur like I do?"

"No."

"Is it because you don't have antlers?"

"No."

"Is it because—"

The boy knew that the monster would just keep guessing until he knew why the boy was grumpy. That's the kind of friend he was.

"I'm grumpy because I'm getting another little sister."

"Ooh," said the monster. "But you already have one of those!"

"Exactly," said the boy.

"Where are you getting the new one?"

"From my mom."

"Why don't you just tell her *no, thank you*?"

The boy had been teaching the monster about manners. It had not been very long since the boy had taken the monster to school and they had a very exciting day—so exciting, in fact, that the boy did not plan to take the monster anywhere else for as long as possible. But just in case they did someday leave the house again, he said it was important for the monster to know good manners.

So far, the monster had learned *yes, please* and *no, thank you* and *excuse me*. That last one was for unexpected body noises and not bumping into people. He knew that for sure. He thought he also knew what *yes, please* and

no, thank you were for, but maybe he
didn't because the boy did not like his
suggestion.

"It's too late for that," the boy said.
"The little sister is coming no matter
what."

"You mean the even littler sister,"
said the monster.

"Yes," the boy groaned.

Just then, they heard a loud banging on their bedroom door. It was the boy's little sister. (The one he had already.) "Who are you talking to in there?" she shouted.

"How am I ever going to deal with *two* of those?" the boy moaned. He pulled a pillow over his head and wrapped it around his ears.

The monster did the same thing. Or
he tried to, but the pillow got caught
on his antlers and ripped and then
there were feathers flying everywhere.

"Ooh," the monster said. He meant,
Oh no and also *Look at that!* Because the
feathers were making a mess and also
they reminded him of snow.

"Want to get out of here?" the
monster asked the boy.

The boy didn't answer. He still had
the pillow wrapped around his ears.

"WANT TO GET OUT OF HERE?"
the monster asked more loudly.

"What was that?" the boy's little
sister shouted. "Who's in there?"

The boy looked up. "Where are we going?" he asked.

"It's a surprise," the monster told him. "Come on."

They crawled under the boy's bed. They closed their eyes and joined hands.

"I hope you know what you're doing," the boy whispered.

"I've been practicing," the monster told him.

And that was true.

Here's another thing that's true: because both of them—the monster and the boy—had their eyes closed, neither one of them saw the boy's little sister peek under the bed. And neither one of them noticed when she crawled underneath to join them.

2.

You are probably wondering what the monster had been practicing.

I know I am wondering that.

What is it, I have been wondering, that monsters do all day while their boys (and girls) are at school?

Do they have dance parties, like stuffed animals do?

Do they take cooking classes and

ballroom dancing lessons, like cats and hedgehogs do?

Do they design fancy outer-space cities, like dogs and guinea pigs do?

Of course you already knew about your stuffed animals and cats and hedgehogs and dogs and guinea pigs. Everyone knows how *those* creatures occupy themselves. But what about monsters?

Well, *this* monster had been practicing several things. He had been practicing his manners.

He had been
practicing
his reading
skills. And
he had been
practicing his
getting small
and getting big again.

He had gotten quite good at all these
things, and he didn't even need to fall
asleep first in order to
make something
small or big
anymore.

big

small

Which is how he knew that he could close his eyes and hold the boy's hand and focus very, very hard and make both of them tiny.

That was his plan. And it worked!

There was just one or two extra things that also happened.

The first was the boy's little sister getting tiny, too.

The second was the appearance of the green door.

3.

"Open your eyes," the monster told the boy.

The boy opened his eyes. He saw the monster next to him, still holding his hand. He saw a huge spaceship nearby and a huge race car in the distance. He saw a strange dark sky over their heads.

"What is this place?" the boy asked.

"It's underneath-the-bed," said the monster.

"Ohhh," the boy said. The spaceship

and race car were toys. The sky was
the bottom of his mattress. He sighed
a sigh of relief. Then he gasped a gasp
of surprise.

"What are *you* doing here?" he
hollered.

The monster turned and saw the
boy's little sister. She was tiny, too.
She was staring at them.

"I remember you from the
kitchen," she said to the monster.

"I remember you, too," the
monster said. He also
remembered what the
boy had told him about
his sister's name, and

his sister's middle name. The monster
slowly walked toward the little sister.
He bent down so his face was near her
belly.

"What's your name?" he said to the
sister's belly.

The belly grumbled.

The monster jumped.

"Do you have any candy?"
the sister asked the monster.

"No," the monster said.

"Is there candy in there?" the sister
asked, and she pointed to the green door.

"Where did that come from?" the boy
said.

The monster looked at the door. It
was a beautiful green, like bright grass
on a warm spring day with no clouds
and birds singing all around. It had
a gold handle that was shining.
Almost . . . glowing. The monster
smiled. "That's the surprise," he
told the boy. "Surprise!"

"You said *surprise* twice," the little sister said.

"Well," said the monster, "that's how much of a surprise it is."

"It's just a door," she said.

The monster shook his antlers. "Oh, no, it's not," he said.

"Okay," she said, "it's a *green* door. With a shiny handle."

"And?" the monster said.

"And . . . if we open it, there's candy?" the sister asked.

"There could be," said the monster.

"Do conversations with him always take this long?" the sister asked the boy.

"Pretty much," he told her. "Let me try."

The boy stood in front of the monster. He looked very seriously into the monster's eyes. "I think the surprise is what's behind the door. I think you want us to go through the door. Is that right?"

The monster hopped from one foot to the other. "Yes, yes!" he said.

"Before we go through the door," said the boy, "will you tell us what's on the other side?"

The monster stopped hopping. "I would like to," he said. "But I can't."

"Why not?" asked the boy.

"Because I forgot," the monster told him.

"Then how do we know it isn't

something dangerous?" asked the sister.

The monster snorted. "Look how beautiful that door is!" he said. "There must be something wonderful behind it! And also," he added, "I have a feeling."

"What kind of feeling?" asked the boy.

"A feeling like a warm, sunny, birdsong day," said the monster.

"Do you trust his feelings?" the sister asked the boy.

The boy looked at the monster. He looked at the door. Then he looked at his sister, and he took the monster's hand in his. "I do," he said. "Let's go."

The sister, the boy, and the monster each took a deep breath and stepped up to the green door. The boy reached out, curled his fingers around the handle, and pressed down.

Nothing happened.

"I think," he said, "it's locked."

locked!

4.

When someone says "surprise!" to you, there's usually a surprise pretty quickly after that. That's sort of how surprises are supposed to work. Hearing the word *surprise* and then having to wait for something to happen is very confusing for your brain.

It would be like if you came home from school and your mother yelled, "Surprise!" and then just kept stirring the pot of soup on the stove. Your brain would probably try to find a surprise somewhere else in the kitchen. Your brain might wonder if there was a surprise *in* the pot of soup, like maybe your mother was pretending to stir soup but really there was a bunch of hamsters in there. Then your brain would start to worry about the pot of hamsters and whether the hamsters were getting too hot, and you'd also probably worry about your mother and why in the name of Jupiter she was stirring hamsters, and you'd get yourself quite excited and knock over your grandmother's antique pickle jar.

That's quite an imagination you've got there.

Remarkable, really.

5.

"It would help if you could remember what's on the other side of the door," the boy told the monster. "If you could remember that, you might also remember how to open it."

The monster nodded. He sat down on the floor and pulled his knees up and wrapped his arms around them, so he looked like a furry ball. With antlers. He shut his eyes tight and squeezed them hard, and he made a kind of deep, growling sound from his belly. He did this for about three minutes, which is a pretty long time even if it doesn't sound like it.

"What are you doing?" the sister finally asked.

The monster opened one eye. "I'm trying to remember," he said.

"Is it working?" she asked.

The monster sighed. "Not really," he said.

"I'm not surprised," she mumbled. When she said *surprised*, the monster remembered something. Not about the green door. About how his surprise for the boy had not worked.

The monster sniffed.

"Uh-oh," the boy said.

The monster sobbed.

"Oh no," the boy said.

The monster howled.

"Stop!" the boy said. "My parents will hear you!"

The monster did not stop. Not even a little bit. The boy looked very nervous.

"You can't make someone stop crying by telling them to stop crying," the little sister said.

"Well, if you're so smart, you get him to stop," the boy snapped.

"Okay, I will," she told him. She sat down next to the monster on the floor.

Even though they were both tiny, the monster was still much bigger than she was. She put her arms around as much of the monster as she could. She squeezed, but gently.

The monster quieted down. He stopped crying. He hiccuped.

"See?" the little sister told the boy. "You can't just tell someone to stop crying." She looked up at the monster. "And you can't make yourself remember by turning into a ball."

"Then how?" the monster asked.

"Retrace your steps?" the boy said. "That's what I do when I lose something."

The monster walked backward around underneath-the-bed. "Like this?" he asked.

"Kind of?" said the boy.

"My mom likes to remember things by telling stories," the sister said. "Lately she's been telling a lot of stories about when we were babies, for some reason."

"I like stories," the monster said.

"What's your favorite?" asked the sister.

"Once there was a monster who loved a boy," the monster said.

"Is there a green door in this story?" asked the sister.

"No," the monster said.

"Then it probably won't help," said the sister.

"You tell one," the monster said.

"Me?"

"Yes, please."

The sister sighed. She looked at the green door. "There better be candy in there," she said. Then she started her story.

Cotton candy clouds

lollipop

jelly bean cars

6.

The Little Sister's Story

This story is about a family.

There was a family with four people in it.

There was a mother and a father and a sister and—

[Here is where the boy interrupted and said, "And a brother, we get it." And the little sister said:]

And another sister. They were a
lucky family because they didn't have
any boys who thought they knew
everything all the time.

["That *is* lucky," said the monster.]

cotton candy

The family lived in a very normal
house where nothing surprising ever
happened.

But there was something the family
didn't know about their house.

They didn't know that their house
was connected to a top secret candy
factory. And the only way to get into
the candy factory was through a
top secret green door. The door was

pretty small, so the mother couldn't
fit through it and the father couldn't,
either. But the sisters could.

There was only one problem. They
didn't have the key to unlock the door.

[Here is where the sister looked at
the monster. He looked back at her. He
was listening very closely to the story.]

They didn't have the secret code to
unlock the door.

[The sister looked at the monster again. He looked at her. Still listening.] They didn't know the secret knock to unlock the— ["What are you doing?" said the boy. "I'm trying to see if anything sounds familiar to him," the sister said. They both looked at the monster. "Yes, please, I'm listening!" he said. "I don't think he knows," said the boy.] The sisters tried to pick the lock, but it didn't work. They tried to knock all kinds of different ways, but it didn't work.

abracadabra! PLEASE! KICK! knock knock!

knock Knock

ump

abracadabra:

ABRACADABRA

THUMP

THUMP!

PLEASE!!!

knock knock

KNOCK KNOCK

ABRACADABRA

KICK!

THUMP!

ick! THUMP Pretty Please? KNOCK KNOCK KNOCK KNOCK!

abracadabra

They whispered lots of different code words through the keyhole, but it didn't work.

"If only someone had a better idea," the sisters said. "We need help!"

["It's audience participation time," the little sister told the monster. "You're the audience. Participate."

"How?" asked the monster.

"Give the sisters another idea," said the little sister.

"Oh," said the monster. "Okay . . ."

There was a long pause.

"They could ring the doorbell!" shouted the monster.

"What doorbell?" asked the boy.

"The one next to the door," said the monster.

The boy and the little sister and the monster all looked at the green door. And there, next to the door— where there hadn't been anything just a moment ago—was a small gold box. And right in the middle of the small gold box was a shiny button.

doorbell

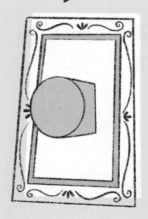

"The end," said the little sister.

"That was a very good story," the monster told her.

"It was okay," said the boy.]

7.

The little sister pushed the shiny button.

It didn't make a sound.

"Try again," the boy told her.

"I know how to press a button!" the little sister said indignantly. But she pressed it again anyway.

Nothing.

She pressed it three more times.

"Maybe it's broken?" the monster suggested.

But just then, the door flew open and a voice said, "Stop that!"

The voice belonged to a monster who looked quite a bit different than the monster in this story. (Well, now there are two monsters in this story. But I mean the monster who was *already* in this story. Before the door opened. I can see that this is going to get confusing. I'm sorry.)

Fortunately, the monster who had just opened the door was wearing a name tag. It said JEFFRICK.

"What do you want?" Jeffrick asked.

"Candy," said the little sister.

"No more sisters," said the boy.

"We want to come in," said the monster.

"Well, which is it?" asked Jeffrick. He sounded annoyed.

The boy and the little sister looked at each other. "We want to come in," they said.

"Yes, please," added the monster.

"You can't," said Jeffrick. "You don't live here."

Now I shall tell you that another good way to remember things is to hear or smell or see something familiar. This is what happened to the monster. Seeing another monster reminded him about why he had wanted to bring the boy through the green door.

"I used to," said the monster.

"Where's your name tag?" asked Jeffrick.

The monster knew that he didn't have a name tag, but he felt all around his fur just in case he *did* have one but it was hiding.

pat

pat

pat

pat

pat

pat

Snack packet

The little sister pointed through the green door. "He left it in there," she said.

Jeffrick bent down and looked very closely at the little sister. "Did he really?"

The little sister did not move. She didn't even blink. "Yes," she said.

Jeffrick stood up. "Okay, then! Let's go!"

The monster walked through the green door. The boy followed him. The little sister followed the boy, and Jeffrick followed her.

"Wow," whispered the monster. "That was scary."

"Yeah," said the boy.

"Your little sister is brave," said the monster. "Is that because she's little?"

"No," said the boy. "It's because she's her. She was born that way."

"Oh," said the monster. "I wonder what your even littler sister will be born like."

The boy sighed. "Just keep walking," he said.

8.

I am getting the feeling that the boy would really rather not have another little sister in his family. I wonder if he'd rather have a little brother. Or a big brother. Those are harder to get, though.

It is not easy when your family changes. A family is like a solar system with a certain number of planets in it, and all the planets can fly around one another without crashing. But then, if a new planet suddenly shows up and wants to join the solar system, things have to change. The old planets have to make room for the new one. They can't just travel along the same orbit they've always had.

It's very complicated.

I bet baby planets are really cute, though.

Mom

Little
Sister
Pluto

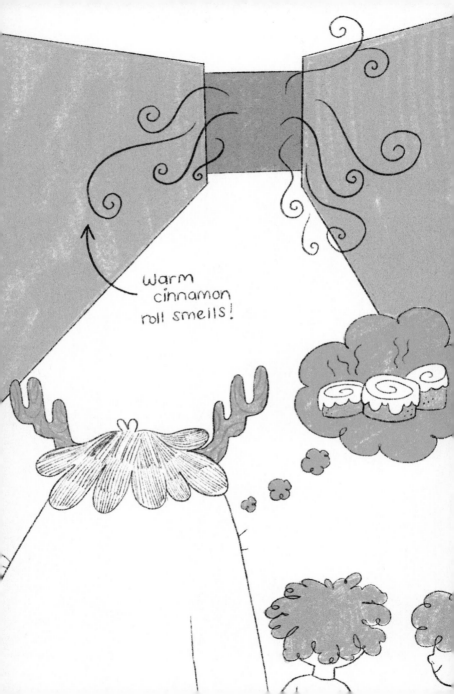

9.

On the other side of the green door, there was a long hallway. The hallway was very bright, as if the sun was shining straight into it, but it didn't feel like being outside. It was very quiet, and it smelled like warm cinnamon rolls.

"What is this place?" the boy asked.

"I don't know, but I love it here," said the little sister.

Jeffrick led them farther and farther

down the hallway. It seemed like the hallway would never end.

"You know what's strange about this hallway?" the monster said.

"Pretty much everything," said the little sister.

"There aren't any doors," said the boy.

"Exactly," said the monster. "It's more like a tunnel."

"Are we underground?" asked the boy.

The monster thought about this. "I don't think so. We went through the green door under your bed, so I think we're . . . in your wall."

"But the wall goes side to side," said the boy. "We walked straight through, and we're still walking straight."

"Are we in a maze?" asked the monster. Suddenly he felt a little bit panicky. Even though it had been his idea to go through the green door, he was starting to worry that it had been a bad idea. Also, he was afraid of mazes.

(All monsters are. Something to do with Greek mythology.)

"We're almost there," Jeffrick said over his shoulder. Then, over the other shoulder, he said, "We're almost there."

"Why did he say that twice?" the monster asked the boy.

"Maybe he wanted to make sure we heard him?"

"I think he's just strange," said the little sister, smiling. "This whole place is strange."

"Are you . . . happy about that?" the monster asked her.

The little sister looked up at him. "Strange is more exciting than regular," she said.

But the monster liked regular. He had gotten used to things being exactly one way, and he liked the way they were. He liked talking to the boy in the morning while he got ready for school, and he liked watching for the boy to come home from school, and he *really* liked listening to the boy read to him at night until they both fell asleep.

He did not like *strange*.

Or *change*, which rhymes with it.

"I like regular," he told the boy.

"Me too," the boy said, smiling.

The monster wondered if he and the boy could find a way to keep things from changing in the boy's family. They had solved some pretty big problems together already. Maybe he could swallow the even littler sister and make her so tiny the boy could barely see her. Or he could learn a magic trick and make her disappear completely.

"I have an idea!" the monster exclaimed.

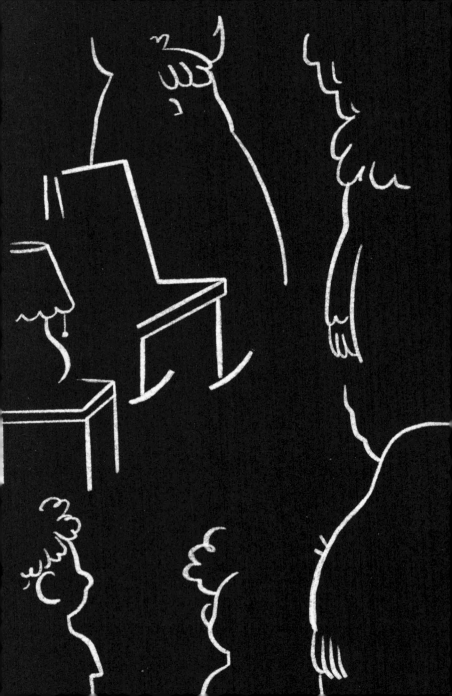

Well, he started to. All he really said was, "I have—!" Because just then, the hallway was over and they were standing in a large square room with dark corners. The dark corners had dark shadows, and one of them had something in it.

Something that growled at them.

Something that started to move toward them.

"No, thank you!" shrieked the monster.

The something gasped. "How dare you say such a rude thing to me!" it said.

And the monster said:

"Mom?"

good manners
pickles

10.

When you are going to visit someone, it is a good idea to call them first. You can make sure they are home and also that they want you to visit and also ask if they want you to bring a jar of pickles to share. That's good manners.

But you probably remember that the monster's mother does not like to talk on the phone, so the monster could not call her first. Maybe if he could have called, he would have remembered why he was bringing the boy (and the little sister) through the green door. Maybe he would have remembered how to get through the green door, too.

It's no use wasting time thinking about could have and would have and should have, however.

Granny Waffleton taught me that.

She even put it on a needlepoint pillow for me.

It's a very long pillow.

"It's no use wasting time thinking about could have and would have and should have, however."

11.

"What a lovely surprise this is!" said the monster's mother. Then she added, "But your manners have become terrible. Don't ever say *no, thank you* to me again."

"Sorry," the monster mumbled.

"Is this really your mom?" the little sister asked.

"Yes," said the monster.

"Wow," said the little sister. "I wish

my mom had horns and curly hair. My mom has curly hair and no horns. And I think she's been eating all my candy because her belly is *huge*."

The monster mother patted her curly hair. "Don't feel bad, dear," she said. "I'm sure your mother has her own gifts."

"Oh, she does," said the boy. "She makes the best pancakes in the universe. And she can run faster than anyone else."

"Not lately," said the little sister. "All she does now is fold tiny clothes and talk to her stomach."

"That sounds very odd," the monster mother said. "Are all your other mothers doing that, too?"

candy!

"We only have one mother," the boy
said.

"What?" cried Jeffrick. Everyone
jumped because they had all forgotten
Jeffrick was even there.

"Well, some families have more than
one, but ours doesn't," said the boy.

"Some families have two fathers and
no mothers at all," the little sister said.

"Huh," said Jeffrick. "Well, as long as there's someone to take care of all the eggs."

The boy and the little sister looked at each other.

Jeffrick became alarmed. "Someone *is* taking care of your eggs, aren't they?"

The little sister shrugged. "I'm pretty sure they're safe in the refrigerator."

And with that, Jeffrick fainted.

"Oh, dear," said the mother monster.

"Is he okay?" the boy asked.

"Why is he so worried about our eggs?" the little sister asked.

"I think I know," the monster said.

You probably noticed how quiet the monster had been for the last few pages. He had not been talking, but he had been listening. And he had been remembering many things about this place behind the green door. Now he turned to his mother.

"I think we should show them the nursery," he said.

12.

After reviving Jeffrick—and assuring him that everyone's eggs were just fine—the monster's mother led them down another hallway. Unlike the first hallway, which had no doors, this one had lots of doors. Each door was a different color. They passed a yellow door and then a blue door and an orange door, and finally they came to a purple door.

"Are you sure?" the monster's mother asked him.

The monster thought about three things. He thought about how the boy shared his room and everything in it with the monster. He thought about how the boy's little sister had helped him calm down outside the green door. And he thought about how much he had learned from the boy and the little sister. "Yes," the monster said. "I'm sure."

She nodded, and Jeffrick pulled a ring of very large keys out of his fur. He unlocked the purple door, and they all stepped through.

They found themselves in an enormous room. The room was full of three things. It was full of gentle, soothing light. It was full of monster mothers. And it was full of very large eggs.

Each egg was about the size of a
pillow, and each one was a different
color. Sky blue, eggplant purple, leaf
green, butter yellow, sunset orange,
and ruby red. The most beautiful colors
there are.

"Ooh," said the monster.

"Ooh," said the boy.

"Whoa," said the little sister. "Are those . . . candy?"

The mother monster laughed. "No, the candy is in a different room. These are our babies."

The boy was amazed. "Monster babies hatch out of eggs?"

"Of course," said the mother monster. "Didn't you?"

"I don't remember," the boy admitted. "I was very young."

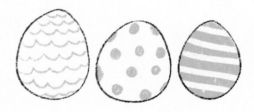

All the monsters in the room were helping take care of the eggs. Some of them were reading stories to the eggs. Some of them were gently rocking the eggs. And some of them were bathing the eggs so their shells were extra shiny.

"Do you think your new little sister will come out of an egg?" asked the monster.

The little sister narrowed her eyes. "What new little sister?"

The boy sighed. "Mom and Dad were going to tell you. But I guess I will. You know how Mom is pregnant?"

The little sister shrugged. "She said she was, but I was in the middle of a game so I fibbed and told her I knew what that meant."

"Well, it means she's having a baby, and they found out it's a girl. We're getting a new sister."

Then a strange thing happened. The little sister's chin started to wobble.

The little sister's eyes started to water.
And the little sister began to cry.

"I don't want to go!" she wailed. "I'll
be better! I'll share the candy!"

"What are you talking about?" the
boy shouted. He had to shout, because
the little sister was making quite a lot
of noise.

The monster put one furry arm
around the little sister. He pulled her
close to his body. His fur was soft
and comforting. It was also good for
muffling loud noises.

Waahh...

"I think," he said to the boy, "she's scared."

"She's never scared," said the boy.

"There's a first time for everything," Jeffrick said. "Granny Waffleton told me that."

WHAT? HOW DOES JEFFRICK KNOW GRANNY WAFFLETON?

That woman is full of surprises.

The little sister sniffled. "I like our family," she said. "Even if our mom doesn't have horns."

"Getting a new little sister doesn't mean we get rid of the old one," the boy told her. "We're adding. Not subtracting."

"I like adding better than subtracting," the monster said. The boy had been trying to teach him about math. Subtraction was . . . not going very well.

"Me too," said the boy.

"Me three," said the little sister. Her belly grumbled.

This reminded the monster of something he had wanted to know for a long time.

"Mom?" said the monster. "What's my name?"

"I have no idea," she said. "Where's your name tag?"

"How can you not know his name?" the little sister scolded.

The mother monster put her furry hands on her furry hips. "Listen, young lady! Do you have any idea how many monsters I've hatched? Thousands! Maybe thousands of thousands! I can't possibly remember all their names. That's why they get name tags. And their name tags are *their* responsibility."

The monster whimpered a little.

"Wow," the little sister whispered. "Moms really do all speak the same language."

The boy put his hand in the monster's fur and scratched his favorite spot. "It's okay," he told the monster. "We'll figure something out." Then he asked the mother monster, "What's *your* name?"

She stared at him. "No one has ever asked me that before."

"Do you need to check your name tag?" the little sister asked.

The mother monster raised a furry eyebrow. "No, I do not," she said, "but you are welcome to see it." She reached into her fur and felt around for a minute. "Ah, here it is," she said.

She held it out so they could read it.

It said—

DEEPAK

TROY

JULIA

POTATO

GABRIELA

GUILLERMO

OLIVE

LEON

ZAYNA

anoosha

carlos

TERRI

CHEESE-LOUISE

ZIG-ZAG

ROCK

Jérémie

TAYLOR

ANDRÉ

BISCUIT

TONIKO

HAEWON

JAMAL

KOFI

Harrington

Mr. Awesome

MALLORY

CALVIN

JESSIE

13.

You know, names are funny things, if you think about it. They're really just words. They're made out of the same letters as every other word, but only certain words get to be names. Why can't any word be a name? Why can't I name someone *Word* if I want to?

Can I?

You seem irritated that I interrupted
the story when I did.

But I had a good reason.

You'll see what it is in a minute.

You trust me, don't you?

grace

BERNIE

WOOF!

FERNANDO

PADDINGTON

KHADIJAH

DELANEY

WOAHHH!!

JULY

LOOPY

PB&J

ISABELLA

MIZUKI

XIAO

Gabriella

ALIYAH

squirrel

jane

JACKSON

ASHLEIGH

HANNAH

MAHAM

CHLOe

JONNY

YUKHI

PAPER

mimi

Mikael

monster
mom's
name tags

14.

After the mother monster showed the monster
and the boy and the little sister her
name tag, she felt wonderful. It had
been so long since anyone had looked
at her name tag, and her name was
so very beautiful that it was lovely to
share it again.

The monster felt less wonderful because seeing his mother's name tag reminded him of how much he wanted a name of his own. And also that he had, apparently, lost his name tag, and he was therefore irresponsible.

The boy and the little sister felt
several different things. They felt lucky
to have seen the place where monsters
are born. They felt tired because it was
the middle of the night and they—
unlike monsters—were not nocturnal.

And they felt just a little bit anxious because they still didn't know what to think about getting a new little sister, even though they had agreed that addition was better than subtraction.

So there were many different feelings swirling around the room together. Then Jeffrick ran in and added another one.

"You have to go home!" he yelled. "Right now!"

15.

It is true that something was happening at the
boy and little sister's house.

It is also true that I missed most of
it because I was still trying to figure out
how Jeffrick knows Granny Waffleton.

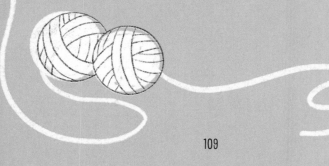

My apologies. I can tell you this

much:

16.

After the monster and the boy and the little sister said goodbye to the monster mothers—all thirty-seven of them!—and came back through the green door, they heard heavy footsteps running toward the boy's bedroom door and their father's voice yelling, "Get dressed, kids! We're going to the hospital!"

While their father ran back downstairs and paid the babysitter, the boy and the little sister got big, but the monster stayed small so he could go with them to the hospital. (He was disguised as a stuffed animal. It was a very good disguise, except for when he needed to sneeze.)

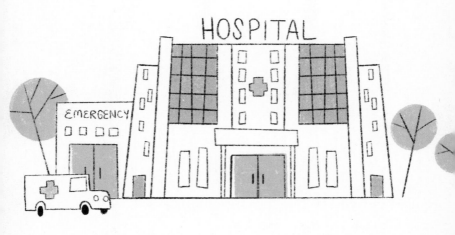

The hospital was very large and
very white. It did not smell like warm
cinnamon rolls, but it did have very
long, straight hallways. The boy and
the little sister (and the monster)
followed their father down one hallway
and then another and then another,
until they came to an enormous
window. On the other side of the
window was a room.

A room full of babies.

The babies were wrapped in fuzzy blankets that were all different colors. Sky blue, eggplant purple, leaf green, butter yellow, sunset orange, and ruby red. The most beautiful colors there are.

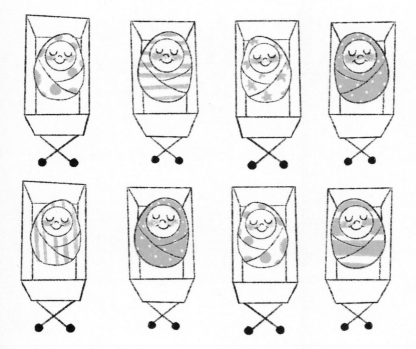

Each baby had its own little bed,
and attached to the end of each little
bed was something very important.

"Name tags," whispered the boy.

"Which baby is ours?" the little
sister asked her father.

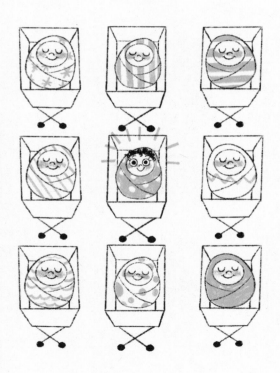

"That one," he said. He pointed to a baby in the very middle of the room. Most of the babies' eyes were closed, but their baby's eyes were wide open. She was wrapped in a fuzzy blue blanket. She was looking right at them.

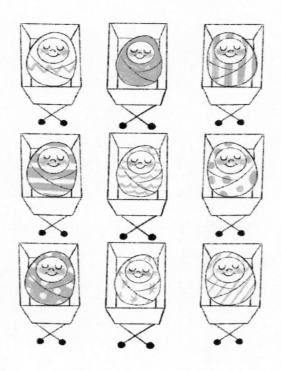

The boy held the monster so he could see.

"Her fur looks just like mine!" the monster whispered.

"Why is her name tag empty?" the little sister asked her father.

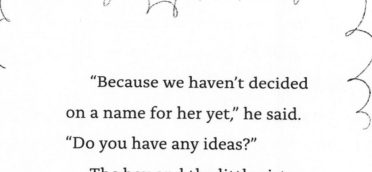

"Because we haven't decided on a name for her yet," he said. "Do you have any ideas?"

The boy and the little sister both thought about the place behind the green door. They thought about mothers and eggs.

They thought about families that are all different but also the same, and about how much nicer addition is than subtraction.

And they thought about the monster mother's beautiful name.

"I think we do," the boy said.

17.

Later that night, the boy and the monster—who was still smaller than usual but not as small as he had been at the hospital— were sitting on the boy's bed. They were talking about their adventure.

"Remember when I couldn't remember how to open the green door and then your sister rang the doorbell and we met Jeffrick and we saw my mother and she showed you the eggs and then we met your baby sister and she looked like me?"

The boy smiled. "Yes," he said.

"Is that why you named her after my mother?" the monster asked.

"No," said the boy. "We just thought your mother's name was a good one to share."

"I didn't know you could share names," said the monster.

"Families do that a lot," the boy told him.

The monster sighed. He was happy that he had gotten to see his mother, but he was sad that she couldn't tell him his name. He really, really wanted one.

He looked at the painting on the wall of the boy's room.

It was a smallish rectangle in a wooden frame. It had five letters and each letter had a little picture next to it. There was a *J* and a jar of jelly. An *A* and an apple. An *M* and a monkey. An *E* and an egg. An *S* and a sock.

"Jelly Apple Monkey Egg Sock," said the monster.

"What?" said the boy.

"Your name," said the monster. "It's so wonderful. I wish I had a name like that."

The boy yawned. He curled his fingers gently into the monster's fur.

"Why don't we share it?" he said.

"Really?" the monster asked.

"Really," said the boy. "That's what families do."

The monster—being nocturnal—was not sleepy, but he curled up next to the boy anyway. "Thank you," he whispered.

"Good night, Jelly," whispered the boy.

The

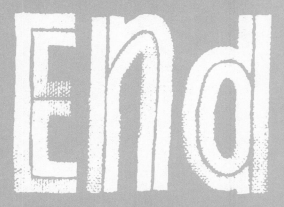

Hannah Barnaby has worked as a children's book editor, a bookseller, and a teacher of writing for children and young adults. Her first novel, *Wonder Show*, was a William C. Morris finalist. Hannah lives in Charlottesville, Virginia, with her family.

hannahbarnaby.com

Anoosha Syed is a Pakistani Canadian illustrator based in Toronto. She has a passion for creating cute, charming characters with an emphasis on diversity and inclusion, and has illustrated many best-loved picture books.

anooshasyed.com